SPOTLIGHT ON OUR FUTURE

CLEAN AIR
AND OUR FUTURE

KATHY FURGANG

NEW YORK

Published in 2022 by The Rosen Publishing Group, Inc.
29 East 21st Street, New York, NY 10010

Copyright © 2022 by The Rosen Publishing Group, Inc.

All rights reserved. No part of this book may be reproduced in any form without permission in writing from the publisher, except by a reviewer.

First Edition

Editor: Theresa Emminizer
Book Design: Michael Flynn

Photo Credits: Cover; (series background) jessicahyde/Shutterstock.com; p. 4 kondrytskyi/Shutterstock.com; p. 5 leungchopan/Shutterstock.com; p. 7 Piupiupics/Shutterstock.com; p. 9 courtesy of Library of Congress; p. 10 Toa55/Shutterstock.com; p. 12 Alfred Eisenstaedt/The LIFE Picture Collection/Getty Images; p. 13 Mirrorpix/Getty Images; p. 14 https://en.wikipedia.org/wiki/Harry_S._Truman#/media/File:TRUMAN_58-766-06_(cropped).jpg; p. 15 https://en.wikipedia.org/wiki/Clean_Air_Act_(United_States)#/media/File:Clean_Air_Act_Signing.jpg; p. 16 Martin Good/Shutterstock.com; p. 17 Harold Cunningham/Getty Images; p. 18 Tanakorn Akkarakulchai/Shutterstock.com; p. 19 ivan_kislitsin/Shutterstock.com; p. 20 Denis Burdin/Shutterstock.com; p. 21 katz/Shutterstock.com; p. 23 Pablo Blazquez Dominguez/Getty Images; p. 24 Killua X/Shutterstock.com; p. 26 lev radin/Shutterstock.com; p. 27 picture alliance/Getty Images; p. 29 (Irsa Hirsi) Mike Jett/Shutterstock.com; p. 29 (Greta Thunberg) Daniele COSSU/Shutterstock.com.

Cataloging-in-Publication Data

Names: Furgang, Kathy.
Title: Clean air and our future / Kathy Furgang.
Description: New York : PowerKids Press, 2022. | Series: Spotlight on our future | Includes glossary and index.
Identifiers: ISBN 9781725323698 (pbk.) | ISBN 9781725323728 (library bound) | ISBN 9781725323704 (6 pack)
Subjects: LCSH: Air--Pollution--Juvenile literature. | Air quality management--Juvenile literature.
Classification: LCC TD883.13 F87 2022 | DDC 363.739'2--dc23

Manufactured in the United States of America

Some of the images in this book illustrate individuals who are models. The depictions do not imply actual situations or events.

CPSIA Compliance Information: Batch #CSPK22. For further information contact Rosen Publishing, New York, New York at 1-800-237-9932.

CONTENTS

WE ALL WANT CLEAN AIR 4

CLEAN AIR AND YOUR BODY 6

HISTORY OF AIR POLLUTION 8

CARS AND POLLUTION 10

AIR AROUND THE WORLD 12

FIGHTING POLLUTION 14

AIR QUALITY IMPROVEMENTS 16

AIR POLLUTION INDOORS 18

CLIMATE CHANGE 20

TAKING ACTION 22

COMPANIES TAKE ACTION 24

GOVERNMENTS TAKE ACTION 26

KIDS TAKE ACTION 28

BREATHING FRESH AIR 30

GLOSSARY 31

INDEX 32

PRIMARY SOURCE LIST 32

WEBSITES 32

CHAPTER ONE

WE ALL WANT CLEAN AIR

Breathe in and then slowly breathe out. If the air you breathe isn't clean, you could become very sick. In fact, we wouldn't even be able to live on Earth if the **atmosphere** became too polluted. People must all play a part in helping keep our air clean and safe.

Air enters our body through the nose and mouth and then moves to the lungs.

There are natural forms of air pollution. We can't always avoid these. Forest fires and volcanic eruptions make the air difficult to breathe. But people add to air pollution too. Picture a city skyline with factory smoke pumping into the air. All that smoke can be deadly. Fortunately, people have made changes over the past 50 or 60 years to make air quality better around the world. Individuals have made a big difference, but more help is needed for the future.

CHAPTER TWO

CLEAN AIR AND YOUR BODY

Did you know that some pieces of pollution can be 30 times smaller than the width of a human hair? That makes it very easy for the pieces to get into your nose, mouth, and lungs.

It's great news that air quality has improved over the past 100 years. However, air pollution is still a very serious problem around the world. Breathing polluted air is linked to many illnesses, including lung cancer and **asthma**. Air pollution causes more than 6.4 million deaths every year. More than 500,000 of those people are children.

Air pollution affects some people more than others. Older people have weaker lungs. Children's lungs are still forming. People who live in cities or near busy highways also experience greater effects of air pollution.

Everyone needs clean air to breathe.

CHAPTER THREE
HISTORY OF AIR POLLUTION

Air quality has been a problem for thousands of years. Since people started using fire, smoke and particles, or pieces, from burned things have created air pollution.

Heat from fires provides the energy we need to do many things, such as cooking. In time, ancient civilizations began to burn matter to remove metals. The process, called smelting, filled the air with thick, heavy smoke.

During the Middle Ages, burning **peat** also affected air quality. Burning peat created the high temperatures needed to make glass and bricks. This process was popular until the mid-1700s, when people began burning coal for energy.

During the **Industrial Revolution**, people built many factories and mills throughout the United States and other countries. The problem of air pollution grew worse.

Workers at the Solvay Process Company plant, pictured here in Syracuse, New York, during the late 1800s, were at risk for getting lung cancer from **asbestos**.

CHAPTER FOUR

CARS AND POLLUTION

We depend on cars to get around every day, but they pollute Earth in several different ways. First, making gasoline includes heating crude oil, a fossil fuel. This oil is a natural resource from Earth that takes millions of years to form. Fossil fuels are nonrenewable resources. This means that once Earth's supply of them is used up, there will be no more available.

The process of turning that oil into gasoline is also harmful to Earth. The oil must be processed through factory systems that pollute the air. When the gasoline is used in cars, the **emissions** pollute the air too. They also add to **greenhouse gases** in the atmosphere. These gases can stay trapped in Earth's atmosphere for thousands of years.

Most cars today run on gasoline made from fossil fuels.

CHAPTER FIVE

AIR AROUND THE WORLD

The 1900s were a time when **industry** grew very fast. For the first half of the century, there were few to no limits on the smoke from factories. This caused several **disasters**.

In October 1948, the normally smoggy air over the mill town of Donora, Pennsylvania, became deadly. The smog from the town's 10 smokestacks was so thick that people had trouble seeing in front of them. Over four days, 20 people died because of breathing issues. Thousands more became ill.

DONORA, PENNSYLVANIA, 1948

This photograph was taken during the Great London Smog of 1952. It shows children playing in the smog.

A similar event occurred in 1952 in London, England. This became known as the Great London Smog. Thick factory smoke became trapped near the ground for five days. About 4,000 people died over a few weeks. These cases of dangerous air pollution made the world take notice.

CHAPTER SIX

FIGHTING POLLUTION

After the disasters in Donora and London, people started taking action. Scientists released a report about the problem. In 1950, President Harry Truman led the first national air pollution conference. It took time, but Congress finally passed the first Clean Air Act in 1963.

HARRY TRUMAN

Because of the Clean Air Act of 1963, the federal and state governments have more control over the standards for car emissions.

The United Kingdom took similar action after the Great London Smog. In 1956, the British government passed its own Clean Air Act. It cut back the amount of coal that factories and people could burn.

These laws were the first of many to help improve air quality and save lives. In 1990, a change to the Clean Air Act addressed issues including acid rain. This is harmful rain with high levels of acid from the atmosphere's gases.

CHAPTER SEVEN

AIR QUALITY IMPROVEMENTS

There have been many successes in air quality control since the Clean Air Act. Organizations such as the United Nations have called for new fuel **technology** that cuts vehicle emissions. Since 1998, these emissions have been cut by 90 percent. Owners of more and more companies are realizing that following pollution laws will help them keep customers.

The headquarters for the World Health Organization, part of the United Nations, is in Geneva, Switzerland. WHO's mission is to work toward the highest possible level of health for all people.

Leaders around the world work together to make lasting changes to air safety laws.

However, there's more work to be done. The United States and Europe have had air quality standards for decades. Other countries haven't been industrialized for as long. For example, China, India, Thailand, Mexico, and Brazil are still building many new factories. These countries have been producing and shipping goods to growing populations around the world. These processes add to the pollution already in the air.

CHAPTER EIGHT

AIR POLLUTION INDOORS

Indoor air pollution is another problem. Tobacco smoke from cigarettes, cigars, and other smoking devices pollutes the air. Tobacco smoke is harmful not just to smokers but also to anyone breathing in the air nearby.

Pollutants such as asbestos and mold are dangerous as well. We may not even know we're breathing them in. Repeated exposure to these pollutants might give people headaches, make them dizzy and tired, or even cause cancer. They may harm the nose, throat, or eyes. It may even take years for symptoms, or signs, to appear.

Other indoor air pollutants include the chemicals in cleaning products and the finishes on new flooring, carpeting, or furniture. When using chemical products indoors, it's important to have as much fresh, clean air available as possible. That may mean keeping windows open or using fans while cleaning.

No smoking inside the room please.

Black mold like this is dangerous to breathe in or touch. It must be removed in a special way.

19

CHAPTER NINE

CLIMATE CHANGE

Air pollution causes another problem besides illness. It's also slowly changing Earth's climate. Throughout the history of the planet, Earth has gone through natural periods of climate change. However, Earth is now in a period of climate change that's the result of human activity. Greenhouse gases in the atmosphere have warmed the climate and damaged air quality.

In 2014, many kids took part in the People's Climate March. They wanted to change the government's laws about the environment.

In Earth's current period of climate change, temperatures around the world have been steadily rising. Five of the warmest years on record have occurred since 2010. Oceans are warming and sea levels are rising. Ice sheets and glaciers are shrinking. Climate change also causes more extreme weather events. Hurricanes and heavy rainfall are causing increased flooding.

CHAPTER TEN

TAKING ACTION

There are many ways to make people aware of the need for clean air. Protests help make people aware of issues. **Boycotts** keep money from going to companies that break pollution laws. Writing to government leaders can also help. It shows how you feel about laws in your town, state, or country.

Education is another way to make a difference. Art can help educate people. In September 2019, British artist Michael Pinsky brought a special art display to the United Nations Climate Action Summit in New York City. Pinsky's *Pollution Pods* is a five-dome sculpture. Viewers walk through it to experience air quality conditions in five places around the world: a Norwegian island; London, England; New Delhi, India; Sao Paolo, Brazil; and Beijing, China.

Each pod in *Pollution Pods* contains facts about the impact of that place's air quality on human health.

CHAPTER ELEVEN

COMPANIES TAKE ACTION

Recently, some companies have tried to help curb climate change. More businesses are looking for ways to use renewable energy, such as solar and wind power. These energy sources give off less carbon dioxide and other greenhouse gases into the atmosphere.

One new process is called carbon capture and storage. It helps cut down on greenhouse gases released into the **environment**. During this process, carbon dioxide is trapped as it's released from a power plant. It's then stored away, usually underground. Many scientists and environmentalists think carbon capture is a promising way to reduce carbon emissions from older factories still burning fossil fuels.

New technologies such as carbon capture can be helpful in developing countries where air quality is especially poor. It can also help older power plants cut emissions.

After carbon dioxide is captured, it's moved, usually in trucks, to other places.

25

CHAPTER TWELVE

GOVERNMENTS TAKE ACTION

Governments have done a lot to help air pollution and climate change. However, there's a lot more they can do. World leaders gather regularly to discuss these problems. Each nation makes its own decisions about how to act.

World leaders met at the United Nations Climate Action Summit in New York City during Climate Week in 2019.

    This is why some nations have stricter air quality standards than others. Countries such as China and India are seeing the economic growth that Europe and the United States had about 100 years ago. The air quality standards in these countries are less firm than the World Health Organization's guidelines.

    Even within the United States, there are differences in air quality. According to the American Lung Association, almost half of the counties in the United States still have air quality below the target standard.

CHAPTER THIRTEEN

KIDS TAKE ACTION

How can kids help air quality and the environment? You can become advocates, or supporters, of environmental issues. When people get involved in making change, governments and businesses take notice.

Young people can play a part in creating change too. The news media has taken notice of Swedish teen Greta Thunberg. She is one among many young people who feel that the adults in power aren't doing enough to address environmental issues.

Some young people have started advocacy groups to bring people together. At 16, American student Isra Hirsi helped start the U.S. Youth Climate Strike. Hirsi and other teens have inspired many students to act and support environmental issues. Their group educates young people about the Green New Deal. This is proposed legislation to address climate change.

ISRA HIRSI

GRETA THUNBERG

In 2019, Thunberg was named *Time* magazine's Person of the Year.

29

CHAPTER FOURTEEN

BREATHING FRESH AIR

Humans have done a lot to address the issue of Earth's air quality. However, more work needs to be done. When people around the world get together for change, their voices become louder.

Some governments and businesses continue to improve air quality. But ordinary people can also make a big difference. Whether people fight for change through protests, education, or even art, the most important thing is to act.

Disasters will still happen, but there are other concerns. In 2020, cases of COVID-19 were worse and more common in areas where air pollution was bad. However, air pollution in some areas decreased because economic activity decreased.

The outlook of the future may be brighter because of the work people are doing today. The young people of today will be the world's leaders tomorrow.

GLOSSARY

asbestos (az-BEH-stuhs) A natural material that doesn't burn and was used in building but can harm people when breathed in.

asthma (AZ-muh) A condition that makes it hard for a person to breathe.

atmosphere (AT-muh-sfeer) The mass of air that surrounds Earth or another planet.

boycott (BOY-kaht) A refusal to buy, use, or participate in something.

disaster (dih-ZAS-tuhr) Something that happens suddenly and causes much suffering and loss for many people.

emission (ee-MIH-shuhn) Something that is given off, or the act of producing that thing.

environment (ihn-VY-ruhn-muhnt) The natural world around us.

greenhouse gas (GREEN-howz GASS) A gas in the atmosphere that traps energy from the sun.

Industrial Revolution (in-DUH-stree-uhl reh-vuh-LOO-shuhn) An era of social and economic change marked by advances in technology and science.

industry (IHN-duh-stree) A group of businesses that provide a certain product or service.

peat (PEET) A soil-like material made of partly broken-down vegetable matter, sometimes the first stage in the formation of coal.

technology (tek-NAH-luh-jee) A method that uses science to solve problems and the tools used to solve those problems.

INDEX

B
Brazil, 17, 22

C
carbon dioxide, 24, 25
cars, 10, 11, 15
China, 17, 22, 27
Clean Air Act (British), 15
Clean Air Act of 1963 (U.S.), 14, 15, 16
climate change, 20, 21, 24, 26, 28
coal, 8, 15
Congress, U.S., 14

D
Donora, 12, 14

E
England, 13, 22
Europe, 17, 27

F
fossil fuel, 10, 11, 24

G
gasoline, 10, 11
greenhouse gases, 10, 20, 24

H
Hirsi, Isra, 28, 29

I
India, 17, 22, 27
Industrial Revolution, 8

L
London, 13, 14, 15, 22
lungs, 5, 6, 9

M
Mexico, 17
Middle Ages, 8

P
People's Climate March, 21
Pinsky, Michael, 22
Pollution Pods, 22

T
Thailand, 17
Thunberg, Greta, 28, 29
tobacco, 18
Truman, Harry, 14

U
United Kingdom, 15
United Nations (UN), 16, 22, 27
United States, 8, 17, 27
U.S. Youth Climate Strike, 28

W
World Health Organization (WHO), 16, 27

PRIMARY SOURCE LIST

Page 9
Solvay Process Company. Photograph. Created by Detroit Publishing Co. Published in 1901. Syracuse, New York. Now kept at the Library of Congress Prints and Photographs Division Washington, D.C.

Page 13
The Great Smog of 1952. Photograph. December 7, 1952. London, England.

Page 15
President Lyndon B. Johnson signing the 1967 Clean Air Act in the East Room of the White House. Photograph. November 21, 1967. Washington, D.C.

WEBSITES

Due to the changing nature of Internet links, PowerKids Press has developed an online list of websites related to the subject of this book. This site is updated regularly. Please use this link to access the list: www.powerkidslinks.com/SOOF/cleanair